-HAUNTED HISTORY-

GETTYSBURG IS HAUNTED!

MARIE MORRISON

PowerKiDS press™

NEW YORK

Published in 2021 by The Rosen Publishing Group, Inc.
29 East 21st Street, New York, NY 10010

First edition

Portions of this work were originally authored by Michael Rajczak and published as *Haunted! Gettysburg*. All new material this edition authored by Marie Morrison.

Editor: Jill Keppeler
Book Design: Rachel Rising

Photo Credits: Cover, Nina B/Shutterstock.com; Cover, pp. 1-32 (background) Slava Gerj/Shutterstock.com; p. 5 Delmas Lehman/Shutterstock.com; p. 7 Everett Historical/Shutterstock.com; p. 9 Raggedstone/Shutterstock.com; p. 10 vkilikov/Shutterstock.com; pp. 11, 17 Jon Bilous/Shutterstock.com; p. 13 Cynthia Farmer/Shutterstock.com; p. 15 Bill Dowling/Shutterstock.com; p. 19 Ed Florentino/Shutterstock.com; p. 21 zef art/Shutterstock.com; p. 22, 29 woodsnorthphoto/Shutterstock.com; pp. 23, 27 George Sheldon/Shutterstock.com; p. 25 rick seeney/Shutterstock.com; p. 26 Historical/Corbis Historical/Getty Images; p. 30 Bob Pool/Shutterstock.com.

Cataloging-in-Publication Data

Names: Morrison, Marie, author.
Title: Gettysburg is haunted! / Marie Morrison.
Description: New York : PowerKids Press, 2020. | Series: Haunted history | Includes index.
Identifiers: LCCN 2019050454 | ISBN 9781725319967 (paperback) | ISBN 9781725319981 (library binding) | ISBN 9781725319974 (6 pack)
Subjects: LCSH: Haunted places--Pennsylvania--Gettysburg--Juvenile literature. | Battlefields--Pennsylvania--Gettysburg--Miscellanea--Juvenile literature. | Gettysburg, Battle of, Gettysburg, Pa., 1863--Miscellanea--Juvenile literature. | Gettysburg National Military Park (Pa.)--Miscellanea--Juvenile literature.
Classification: LCC BF1472.U6 M6875 2020 | DDC 133.1/2974842--dc23
LC record available at https://lccn.loc.gov/2019050454

Manufactured in the United States of America

CPSIA Compliance Information: Batch #CSPK20. For further information contact Rosen Publishing, New York, New York at 1-800-237-9932.

CONTENTS

History and Mystery

The fields and hills around Gettysburg don't look like the sort of place to hold so many ghost stories. Neither do the streets in the town, with its old homes, businesses, and college buildings. However, some call this Pennsylvania town and the surrounding countryside one of the most haunted spots in the United States...and it all comes down to three days in July 1863.

Thousands of people died during those three days in Gettysburg, as the Union and the Confederacy clashed in one of the bloodiest battles of the American Civil War. And today, thousands of people a year visit the 9 square miles (23.3 sq km) of the Gettysburg National Military Park, walking where soldiers fought and died to preserve the United States. It's no wonder that ghost stories abound there.

The Gettysburg National **Cemetery**, part of which is shown here, holds the gravesites of more than 6,000 veterans, not just those from the Civil War battle.

THE WAR AND THE BATTLE

The Battle of Gettysburg took place from July 1 to 3, 1863, a little more than two years after the American Civil War began. The 11 states of the Confederacy, fighting in large part to preserve slavery, had **seceded** from the United States, and the remaining states of the Union were fighting against secession. By mid-1863, both sides had already fought a number of battles and lost many soldiers and **civilians**.

The first half of 1863 hadn't been going well for the Union. After his army defeated a Union army at Chancellorsville, Virginia, Confederate General Robert E. Lee decided to invade the North. Armies from both sides met in southern Pennsylvania, in what turned out to be the largest battle on U.S. soil to date.

SPOOKY STUFF

The Battle of Gettysburg is largely considered the turning point in the Civil War. It was also the bloodiest battle.

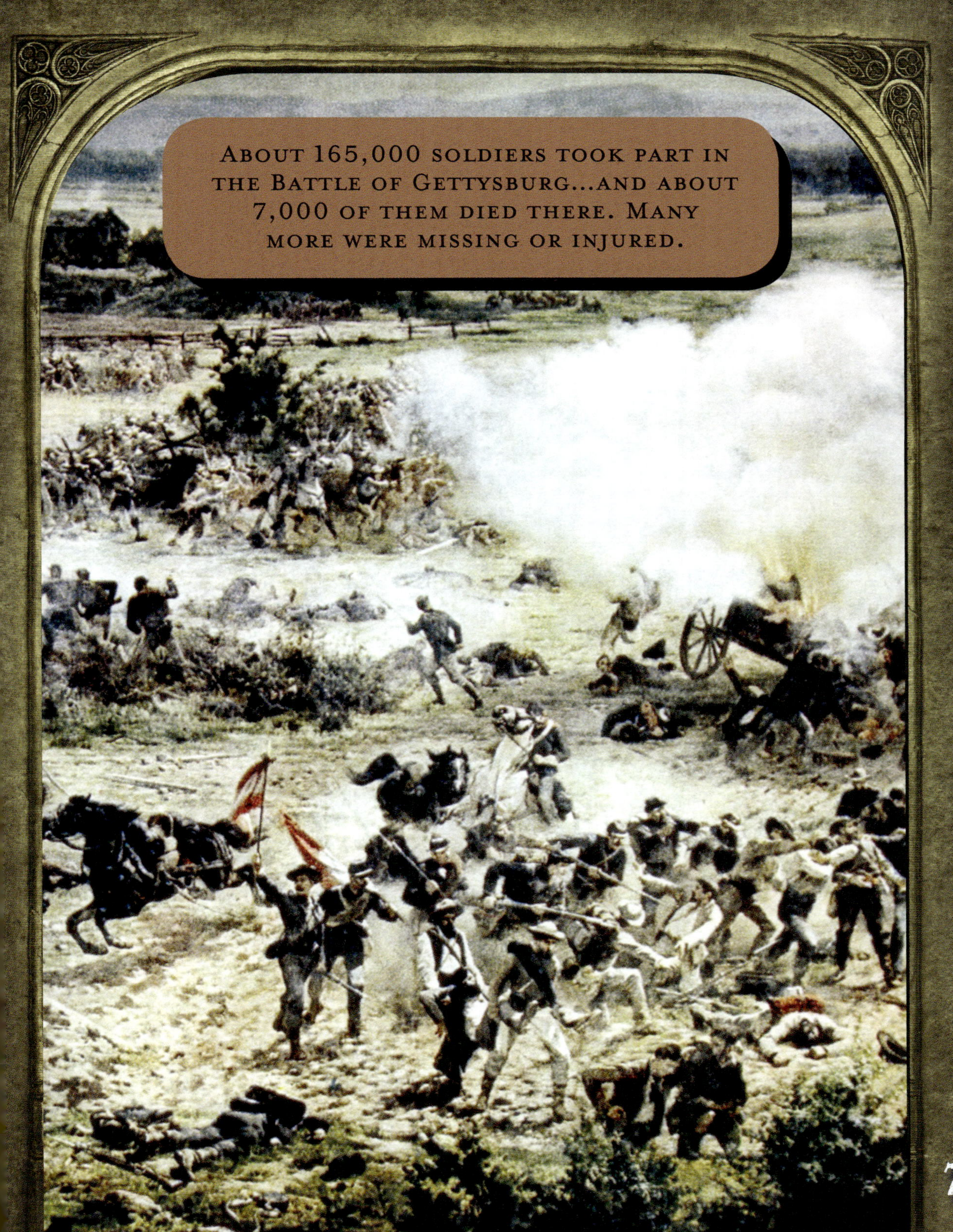

About 165,000 soldiers took part in the Battle of Gettysburg...and about 7,000 of them died there. Many more were missing or injured.

THE ORBS HAVE IT?

Many people have reported taking photographs or videos of odd **orbs** at the Gettysburg battlefield and in the nearby town. Some believe these glowing specks of light show that spirits are present. Sometimes, they're said to be **psychic** energy. Other people see blurry figures or streaks of light—said to be ghosts—in their pictures.

While it's hard to say what some of the mysterious shapes are, many scientists and photographers have an explanation. When light from a camera flash reflects off tiny (and invisible to the human eye) particles in the air, an orb may show up in the resulting photo. Dust, pollen, tiny bugs, droplets of water, or snowflakes can cause orbs. Windows, mirrors, and other reflective surfaces can cause streaks or blurs.

PHOTOGRAPHS CAPTURE ORBS WHEN IT'S DARK—SUCH AS AT NIGHT OR IN A DARKENED BUILDING—BECAUSE LIGHT BOUNCES OFF THEM. OR WHO KNOWS? THEY COULD BE GHOSTS.

A GHOSTLY GENERAL

Of course, locations on the battlefield are among the places most rumored to be haunted. The hill called Little Round Top was the site of fierce fighting on the second day of the battle. Union soldiers held the site despite many Confederate attacks, keeping the other side from overrunning the left side of the Union army.

Years after the battle, a story lingers about how the 20th Maine Division was directed to Little Round Top by a mysterious man in an old-fashioned uniform, riding on a white horse. The division arrived in time to successfully defend the hill. Stories say the soldiers claimed the man looked like George Washington. In some **versions** of the tale, the ghostly general reappears to lead a Union charge at Little Round Top itself.

George Washington died in 1799, long before the Battle of Gettysburg. He's buried at Mount Vernon, Virginia, far from the battlefield.

-A Talk with a Ghost-

People working on the 1993 movie *Gettysburg* hired reenactors to serve as extras while they were filming at the battlefield. One battlefield ghost story says that one group of these extras were talking one day during a break when a old man in a Union uniform approached them, chatting with them and giving them some **ammunition**. According to the story, the bullets wound up being real Civil War ammo—and the old man had vanished!

Little Round Top

THE DEVIL IN THE DETAILS

Devil's Den is a rightfully spooky name for a spooky spot on the Gettysburg battlefield. This area is just downhill from Little Round Top. It's a maze of large boulders that provided cover for soldiers from both sides. There was much fighting at this spot as well on the second day of the battle, and some people say it's one of the most haunted spots on the battlefield. About 2,600 men died there.

Visitors say they've heard drums and gunshots at the site. Some even say things have been pulled from their hands by an unseen attacker! At least one tourist has reported meeting someone who seems to be a reenactor there and taking a photo with him—only to have him missing in the image.

SPOOKY STUFF

A creek that ran between Little Round Top and Devil's Den **allegedly** got the name Bloody Run because it ran red with blood after the battle.

DEVIL'S DEN HAD ITS CREEPY NAME WELL BEFORE THE BATTLE OF GETTYSBURG.

-GHOSTLY GRUDGE-

Devil's Den visitors have reported that their cameras and their camera batteries seem to drain or fail suddenly while they're at the site. **Paranormal** investigator Mark Nesbitt has said that he has an idea about why. Just after the battle, a Civil War photographer apparently moved one soldier's body from place to place on the battlefield to take photos. Perhaps the soldier's spirit still blames photographers today!

A MOST HELPFUL SPIRIT

You probably wouldn't think a wandering spirit at a site such as Gettysburg would be too good-natured, but at least one is very helpful, even today. The so-called Helpful **Hippy**, stories say, appears around the rocks of Devil's Den. He's allegedly clad in raggedy clothes, with a floppy hat, long hair, and bare feet. Visitors say he's appeared when they're lost or uncertain about direction, saying something like "What you're looking for is over there," and vanished again.

The ghost may be the spirit of a Texan soldier. One story says he appeared to a woman wearing a University of Texas sweatshirt, pointed at it, and said "First Texas" before vanishing again. Other stories say that he's offered photography advice to tourists as well!

The helpful ghost near Devil's Den apparently wears the clothing worn by a unit of soldiers from Texas who took part in the battle.

PENNSYLVANIA HALL

Many college **campuses** in the United States have ghost stories—but Pennsylvania Hall at Gettysburg College may have them all beat. The college was founded in 1832, only 31 years before the battle. While the battle was going on, Pennsylvania Hall served as a field hospital—and a **morgue**—for soldiers from both sides.

As the stories go, at one point in more modern history, two college staff members were taking the elevator in the hall down to the first floor late one night. However, it didn't stop there and continued to the basement. And when the doors opened, the two stared out at a scene from July 1863, with wounded and dying soldiers everywhere and doctors and nurses trying to save them.

SPOOKY STUFF

Stories also say that a ghostly soldier sometimes stands at the top of Pennsylvania Hall, looking north.

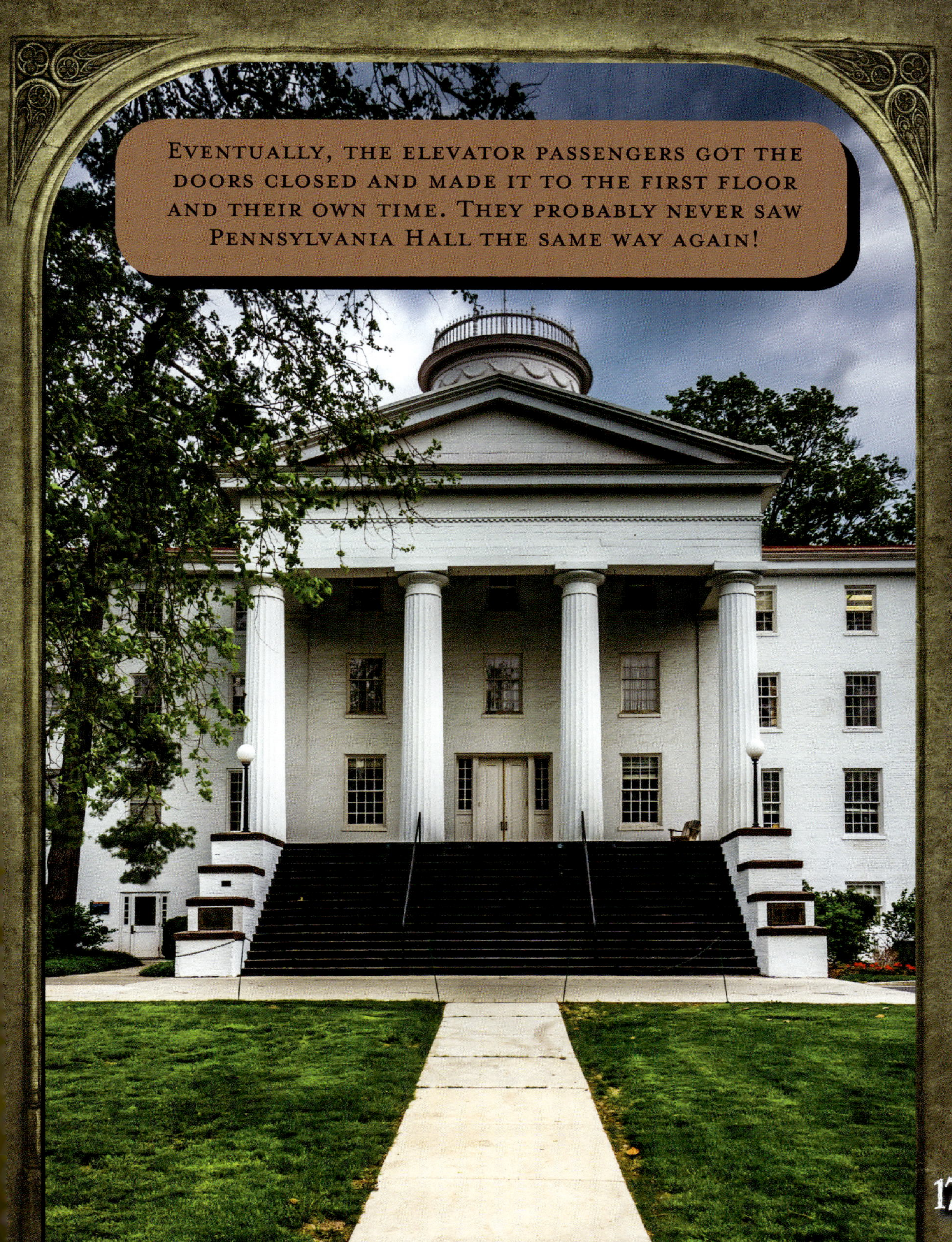

Eventually, the elevator passengers got the doors closed and made it to the first floor and their own time. They probably never saw Pennsylvania Hall the same way again!

OVER TROUBLED WATERS

When you think of haunted structures, a bridge might not be the first thing to come to mind. However, the Sachs Covered Bridge southwest of Gettysburg, built in 1852, is the site of many rumors and tales of ghosts and hauntings. Soldiers from both the Union and the Confederacy used it before and during the battle. Confederate soldiers also crossed it in retreat after they'd lost.

Many soldiers in the retreat would have been badly injured when they crossed the bridge. Perhaps that's why people report hearing the cries of the wounded there even now. Visitors have also reported hearing gunfire at the bridge, sensing cold spots or a feeling of great sadness, and even seeing ghostly men in uniform or an eerie, heavy mist.

Visitors can't drive across Sachs Covered Bridge these days, but they can walk across it. The bridge is about 100 feet (30.5 m) long.

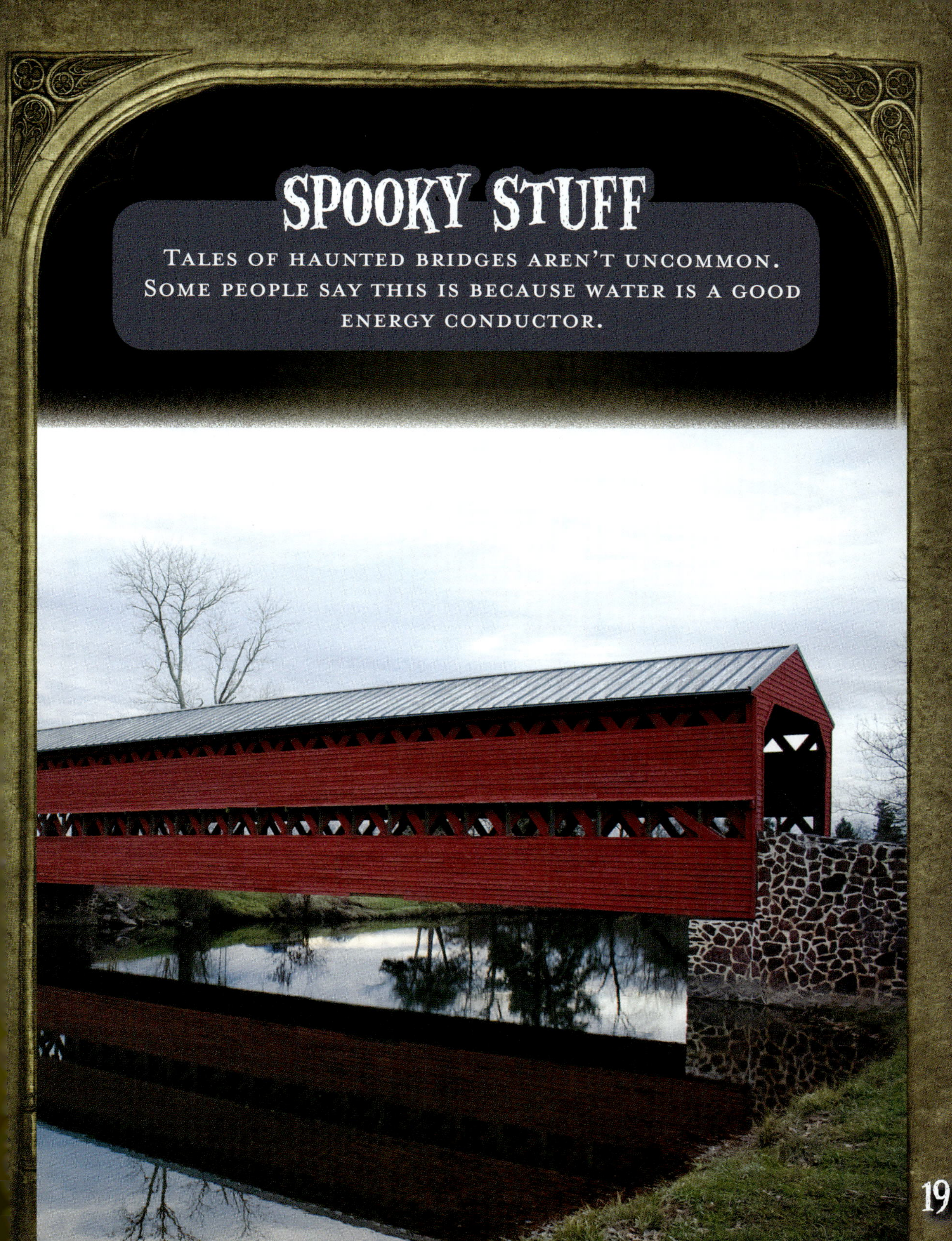

SPOOKY STUFF

Tales of haunted bridges aren't uncommon. Some people say this is because water is a good energy conductor.

HOMES AND HAUNTS

The Battle of Gettysburg didn't stay on the battlefield. In fact, Confederate forces drove some Union troops right through the town on the first day. Townspeople had to hide in their homes as soldiers shot at each other right outside. The fields and hills where there was so much fighting were often visible from Gettysburg's streets. It must have been very scary for this small town of about 2,400 people.

After the battle, things weren't much better. Wounded soldiers filled buildings throughout the town, including churches, the courthouse, and many homes. There were so many bodies that residents sometimes put peppermint oil under their noses to help with the stink. Residents worked for days to cart the **corpses** away and bury them.

SPOOKY STUFF

One story tells of a carpenter's shop where doctors operated on soldiers after the battle. They allegedly tossed the arms and legs they removed through a window, creating a grim pile outside.

During the Civil War, cavalry units—soldiers who rode horses—were very important. It's not surprising that there would be stories of ghost horses at Gettysburg as well.

-Four-Legged Ghosts-

As many as 5,000 horses and mules also died at the Battle of Gettysburg. Some people believe some of these animals still haunt the battlefield as well. Sometimes visitors report seeing ghostly soldiers still mounted on their loyal steeds. They claim to hear ghostly neighing or the sounds of hooves at Sachs Covered Bridge or elsewhere around the town and battlefield.

Many homes in and around Gettysburg are said to be haunted. Today, a number of them are hotels and inns that tourists can visit and stay in. Others are stops on the many ghost tours available.

The Farnsworth House Inn, built in 1810, might be among the most famous. There are more than 100 bullet holes still in its walls. Confederate sharpshooters allegedly took shelter there, and one of them may have killed the only civilian victim of the battle. Tales say the ghosts of both these sharpshooters and wounded Union soldiers remain there. The Gettysburg Hotel, established in 1797; the Cashtown Inn just outside Gettysburg; and the Baladerry Inn, a former field hospital, are other sites rumored to have ghostly guests in addition to the living ones.

DOBBIN HOUSE TAVERN

-Dobbin House Tavern-

The Dobbin House, built in 1776, is another of Gettysburg's historic buildings. The site is on the National Register of Historic Places. It's across the street from the location of President Abraham Lincoln's Gettysburg Address, and it's believed to have been a stop on the Underground Railroad. In fact, stories say that the ghosts of both the abolitionist owner and former slaves still walk its halls today.

The Gettysburg Hotel, shown here, has many ghost stories, including those of a dancing woman in the hotel ballroom, a Union soldier, and a nurse named Rachel.

WHERE THEY REST (OR NOT)

Reports say that Gettysburg was a frightful place after the battle, with unmarked, shallow graves all over. Rain had washed away the dirt from the top of some of the graves, leaving the limbs of the dead poking out. The smell was horrible. The Pennsylvania governor and others worked to create a cemetery for the Union soldiers who'd died, buying land and more thoroughly burying the bodies.

More than 3,500 Union soldiers are buried at this Gettysburg National Cemetery, which was dedicated in November 1863 even though the burials weren't yet completed. People have reported seeing a mysterious, low-lying fog at the site, as well as orbs and streaks of light. Others say they've seen ghostly soldiers or felt like someone was watching them.

Many monuments stand at the Gettysburg National Cemetery, including the Soldiers' Monument, shown on page 25.

SPOOKY STUFF

A few Confederate soldiers are buried at the Gettysburg National Cemetery, but most bodies were moved to cemeteries in the South during the 1870s.

-Four Score and Seven Years Ago-

President Lincoln delivered his famous Gettysburg Address at the dedication of the national cemetery on November 19, 1863. The main speaker, a man named Edward Everett, spoke for two hours that day. Lincoln spoke for about two minutes, but we still remember his words today. He wasn't quite correct when he said, "The world will little note, nor long remember what we say here, but it can never forget what [the Union soldiers] did here."

JENNIE'S GHOST

Only one civilian died during the Battle of Gettysburg: a 20-year-old woman named Mary Virginia Wade. She's now usually called Jennie, though during her life she was called Ginnie. She, her mother, and her brothers were visiting her sister, who had a new baby, at her sister's home in the town of Gettysburg. Wade was kneading bread dough in the kitchen when a bullet struck her in the heart on the third day of the battle. She died instantly.

JENNIE WADE

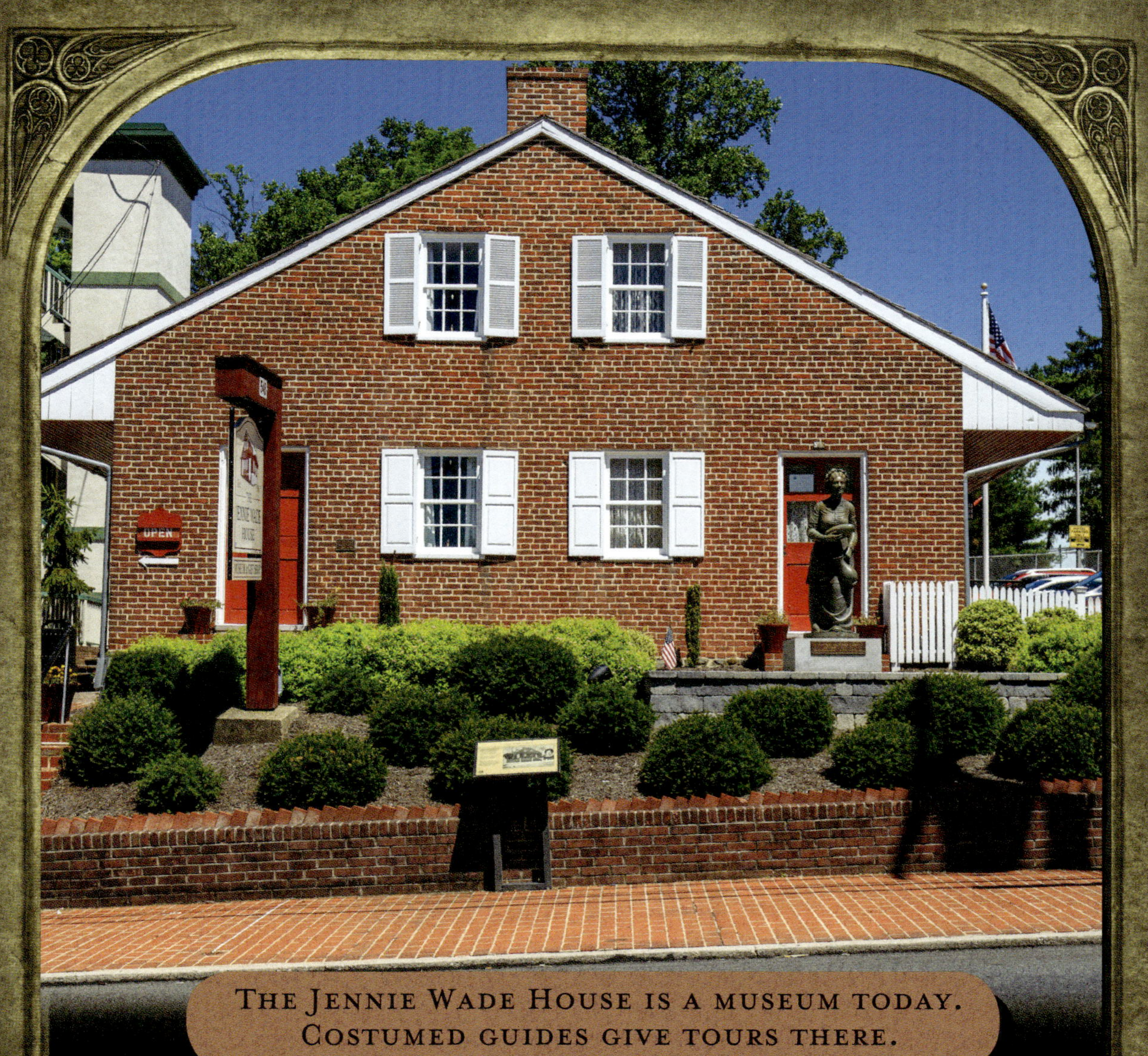

THE JENNIE WADE HOUSE IS A MUSEUM TODAY. COSTUMED GUIDES GIVE TOURS THERE.

Today, people can visit the Jennie Wade House in Gettysburg, although it's actually the house that belonged to her sister. Tales say she's still there in some ways, baking ghostly (but delicious-smelling) bread and going about her chores. Some people say they've even captured her in photographs.

THE BLOODSTAINED FARMHOUSE

During the time of the Gettysburg battle, the Lady family owned a 146-acre (59 ha) farm near the battlefield. As gunfire started, the family left the farmhouse, and on July 2, Confederate soldiers took it over as a staging area for an attack on Culp's Hill. As the battle raged on, the house and barn became a field hospital for men injured in the attack.

Today, the Gettysburg Battlefield Preservation Association owns the farm, where both buildings still stand. The GBPA offers tours, camping, and living history events there. Visitors can still see the bloodstains from the wounded soldiers on the floorboards, and initials carved by Confederate soldiers in the barn. Stories say that the ghost of a general and his men linger there as well.

The Daniel Lady farm isn't the only one said to be haunted in this area. There were many farms around Gettysburg in 1863.

THE WEIGHT OF HISTORY

Whether you believe in ghosts or not, there's no denying that the sense of history is strong on the battlefield and in the town of Gettysburg. Events in this once-quiet location changed the course of the war and had a huge effect on U.S. history. Thousands of people lost their lives here, and the weight of that grim history remains, to some extent, in the historic fields, hills, and homes.

If you have the chance to visit Gettysburg, remember that history. Stand on Little Round Top and imagine what it would have been like to see Confederate soldiers rushing up the sides toward you. Visit one of the former field hospitals and consider how doctors and nurses worked to save lives. Close your eyes in the quiet cemetery—and remember Lincoln's important words.

GLOSSARY

allegedly: Said to have happened but not proven.

ammunition: Bullets, shells, and other things fired by weapons.

campus: The area and buildings around a college or another school.

cemetery: A place where the dead are buried.

civilian: A person not on active duty in the military.

corpse: A dead body.

hippy: A person, often young, who rejects established social customs. Often refers to young people of this sort during the 1960s and 1970s, with long hair and casual clothes.

morgue: A place where dead bodies are kept.

orb: Something shaped like a ball.

paranormal: Not able to be explained by science.

psychic: Relating to supernatural abilities, energy, or knowledge.

secede: To leave a country and become a new, independent country.

version: A form of something that is different from the ones that came before it.

INDEX

WEBSITES

Due to the changing nature of Internet links, PowerKids Press has developed an online list of websites related to the subject of this book. This site is updated regularly. Please use this link to access the list: www.powerkidslinks.com/haunted/gettysburg